MICHAEL'S LOST WORDS

Michael's Lost Words

by Cameron Epperson and Margaret Mayes

Illustrated by Jen Theen

PALMETTO
PUBLISHING

Charleston, SC
www.PalmettoPublishing.com

Michael's Lost Words
Copyright © 2021 by Cameron Epperson and Margaret Mayes

First Edition

Hardcover ISBN: 978-1-68515-117-1
Paperback ISBN: 978-1-68515-167-6

This book is dedicated to:

Christy and Jimmy Epperson
and parents who advocate
for their kids every day.

2021

Thank you for purchasing this book. Cameron and I imagined it as a read aloud story for teachers and parents to share with their children. We hope our story will help to promote understanding of, and appreciation for, those who live with verbal dyspraxia/apraxia.

Michael's Lost Words

Hi! My name is Michael and I
have a secret superpower.

But I'll tell you about that later.

Right now, I'll share some other stuff about me.

I love skateboarding and riding my dirt bike with my dad and friends!

I also like making videos. I want to be a YouTuber when I grow up, and make dirt bike videos to show people how to ride.

And I want to have a store with my dad.

We will have dirt bikes and four wheelers on one side, and skateboards and equipment on the other side.

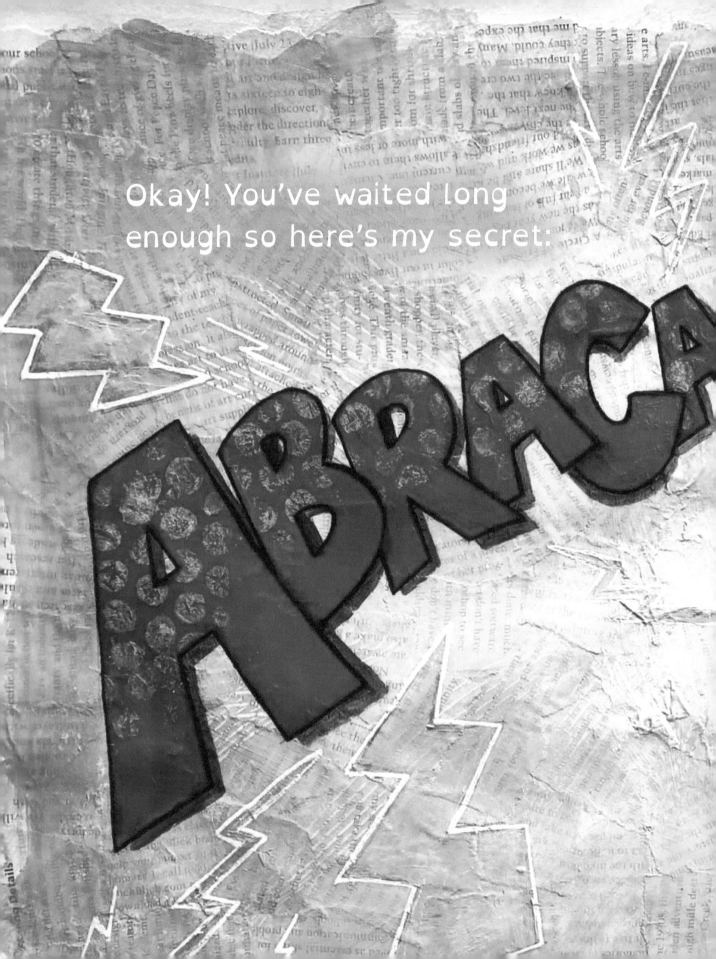

Okay! You've waited long enough so here's my secret:

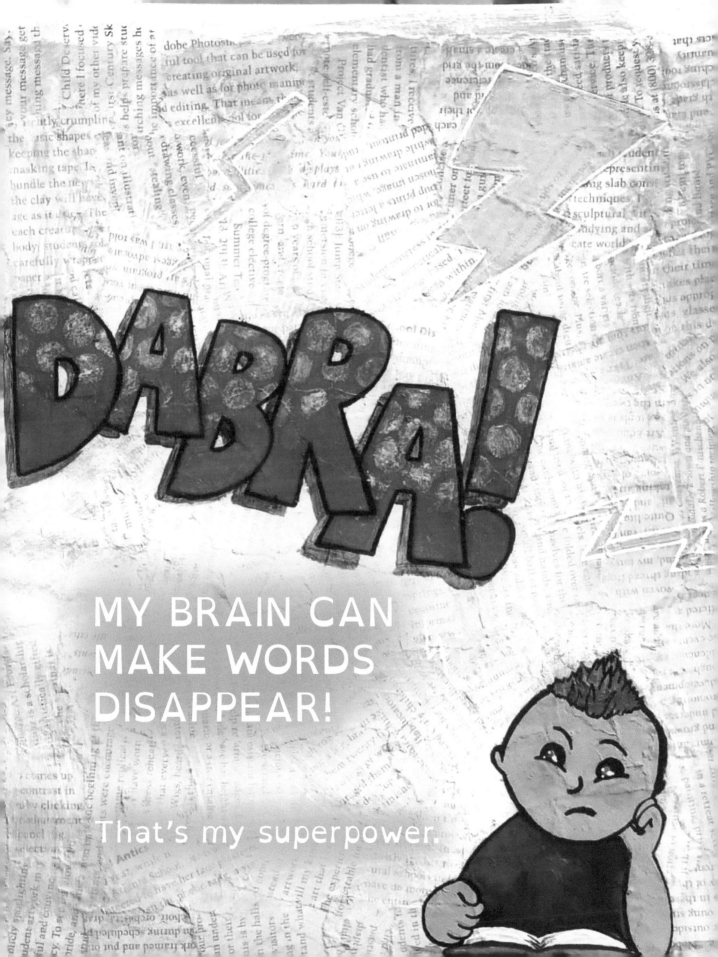

The words get lost between the page and my brain!

(So... I kinda hate reading.)

My brain doesn't send and receive messages the ordinary way.

I think I'm reading words right.
They sound good to me!

Sometimes, words get lost
between my brain and my mouth.

I think I'm saying them just fine.

But sometimes I say the words
wrong.

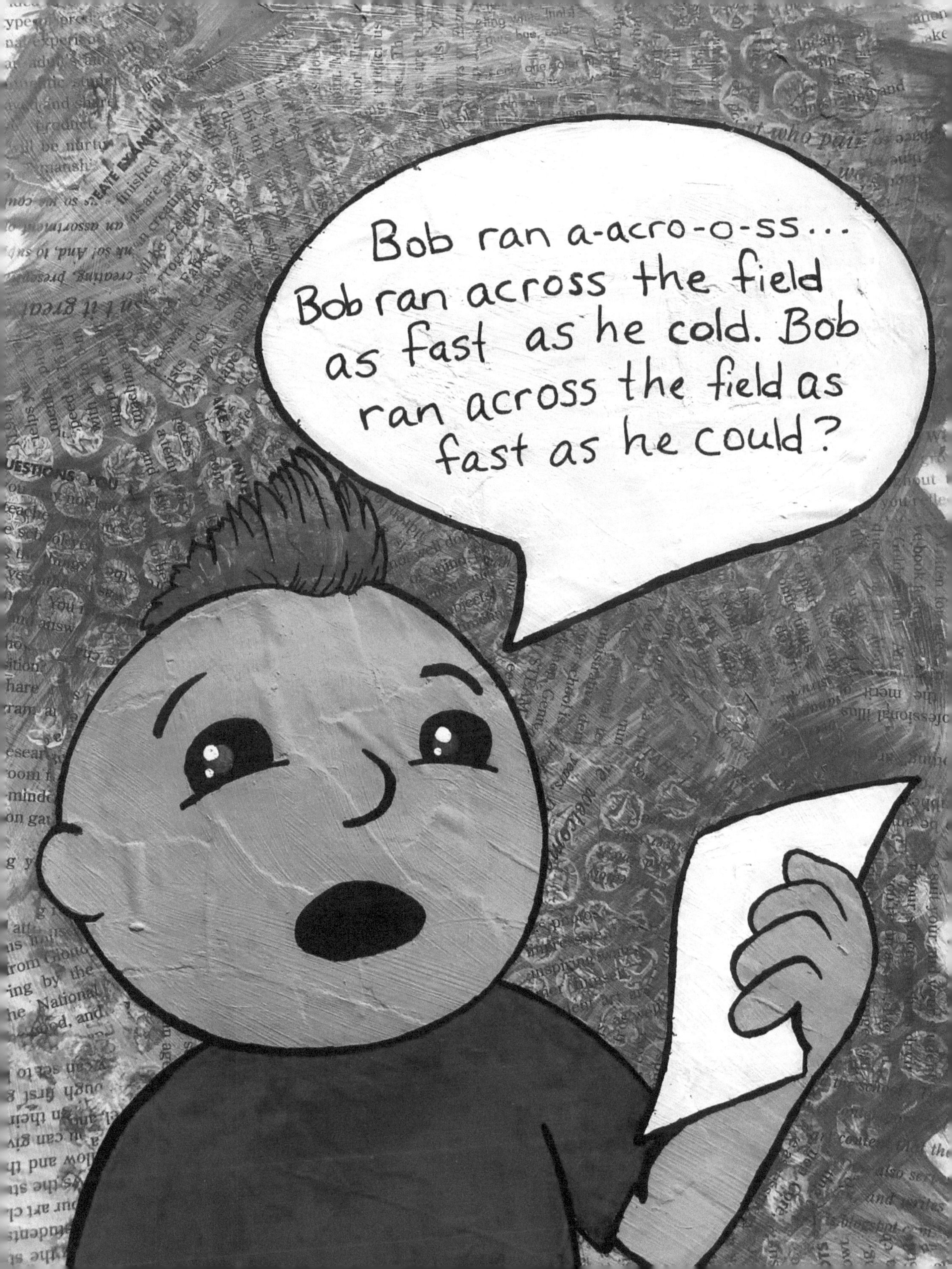

Tuesday, October 9th
Today's Word: challenge
Don't forget:
- Homework due Friday
Raise your hand if you'd like to read next!

So ... this speech thing I have is called verbal (vur bl) dyspraxia (dis prak see uh).

I just call it speech problems.

My brain is fine, but it works in a different way than other people's brains.

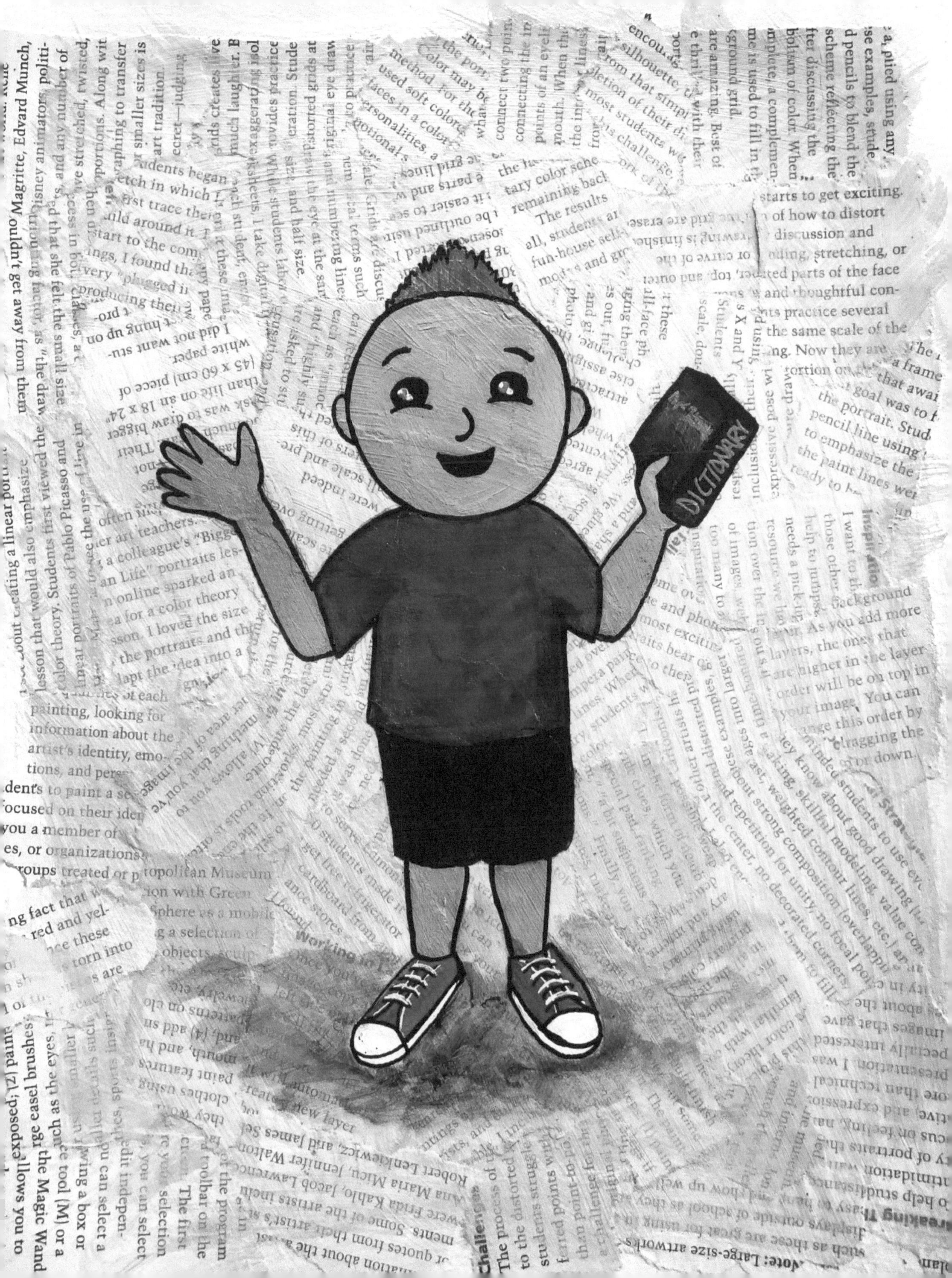
DICTIONARY

When kids ask me, I tell them I was born this way.

So please don't laugh when I say words differently.

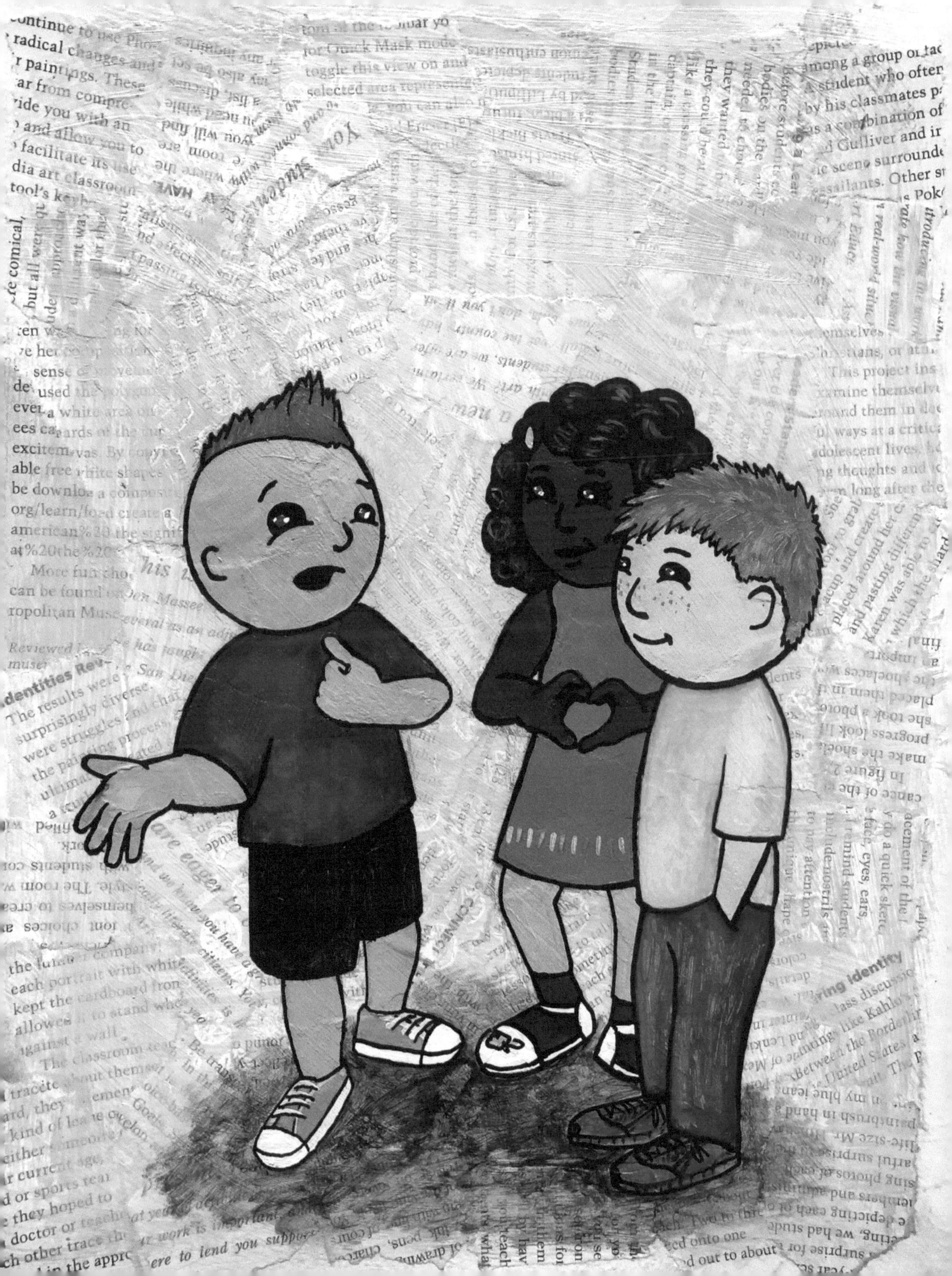

It's all good...

I only want to be me

and for I for you to be you.

Bye for now...
I am going out
dirt biking!

THE END

EPILOGUE

Dyspraxic students need:
- a buddy to help them remember what the teacher said;
- to move around;
- to be reminded of getting things (like supplies or gloves and backpack);
- friends who won't laugh when they can't say words or spell correctly);
- to be accepted for who they are;
- to be included in class activities.

This book reflects Cameron's experiences. Other dyspraxic students may experience more or different learning/body control issues.

Special thanks to Gail Roberson L.P.C. who encouraged me to use my years of knowledge in education to step out in a real and practical way to continue my passion for children and reading.

Much love to my sisters Myra N. Kerr and the late Marilyn K. Mayes.

Many thanks to Joi Hazelrigg, Lynne Dempsey, and Janice Switzer, who read and offered advice from an educators' perspective.

Thank you to our illustrator, Jen Theen, who made our words come to life.

Much love to Blue Kerr, who guided me through the maze of technology that frustrates me so!

PRODUCTION TEAM

Members: Michaels Zans, Lindsay Herbst, Joi Hazelrigg, Natalie Long, Elisha Stevenson, Margaret Barrier, John Hutton, Jennifer Lynn Mobley, Jennifer Dick, Frances Curry, Kristie Rose, Christine Foster, Laurie Doty, Jill Fields, Ginnie Teachout, Brenda Odell, Jennifer Mack, Emaley Mack, Shirley Felz, Anonymous.

Bronze members: Brittnie Thompson, Jocelyn Rowen, Ronia G. West, Alan Bruce Lindgren, Ashley Stolte, Judy Huiffus, Anonymous.

Silver members: Anita Henderson, Myra Kerr, Heather W., Jessica Fields, Vickie Gabbert.

Gold members: Linda Barrier, Gail Barrier.

Producer: Linda Hueffmeier.

REFERENCES

Boon, M. *Understanding Dyspraxia. A Guide for Parents and Teachers*, Jessica Kingsley Publishers 2001.

Boon, M. *Can I Tell You About Dyspraxia? A Guide for Friends, Family and Professionals.* 2014